Holly & Mac

Bill Condon
Illustrated by Gus Gordon

 sundance

Published by
Sundance Publishing
234 Taylor Street
Littleton, MA 01460

Copyright © text Bill Condon
Copyright © illustrations Gus Gordon
Project commissioned and managed by
Lorraine Bambrough-Kelly, The Writer's Style
Designed by Cath Lindsey/design rescue

First published 1997 by
Addison Wesley Longman Australia Pty Limited
95 Coventry Street
South Melbourne 3205 Australia
Exclusive United States Distribution: Sundance Publishing
ISBN 0-7608-1924-6

Printed In Canada

Contents

*To Patricia Bernard, lover of dogs,
terrific writer, and good friend.*

Chapter 1

Holly Makes a Mess

Mac could hardly believe what he saw when he came home.

His good shoes were torn to shreds.

The laundry had been ripped from the clothesline.

There were paw prints on the freshly painted kitchen floor.

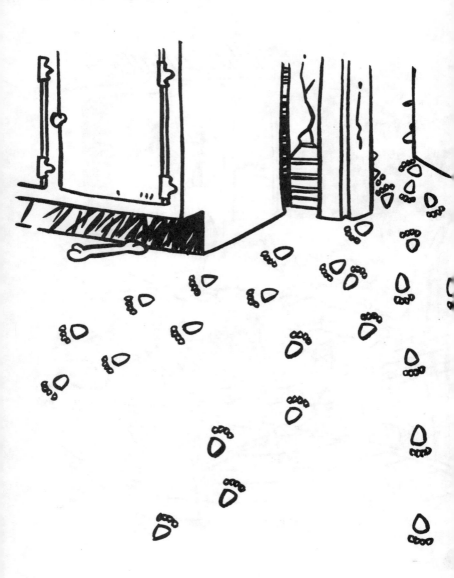

And Holly, Mac's dog, was curled up,
sound asleep, on Mac's favorite chair.

"That trouble-making pooch has gone too far this time!" Mac thundered, as the dog opened her eyes and yawned.

Mac dangled his now not-too-good,
crumpled shoes in front of Holly's eyes.
"Why not pick on an old pair?"

Holly licked Mac's hand.

"This is too much. You're in big trouble! And what are you doing in my chair? You know I don't like *your* fleas mixing with my fleas — it's not hygienic."

Holly bounded from the chair and scurried out of the room.

"You should be ashamed of yourself!" Mac called after her.

In a flash Holly came tearing back, this time holding her leash in her mouth.

Mac let out a deep sigh as Holly's tail waved back and forth like a windshield wiper stuck on high speed.

"You do all these rotten things and then you expect to be taken for a walk — I can't believe it."

Holly dropped the leash at Mac's feet and barked impatiently. Mac looked at the damage and then back at Holly, his one friend in the world.

"You think you're the boss around here, don't you?"

Holly nodded.

"Well, if you don't start behaving, I'll trade you in for a Labrador retriever! A Labrador wouldn't misbehave like you do."

Holly wasn't impressed. After years of loyalty and friendship, Mac was going to use her as a trade-in!

She couldn't understand why he was so angry. How was she to know the floor had just been painted? He hadn't put up any signs to warn her. And those shoes he'd made such a fuss about — she'd only been trying to clean them.

And he hadn't even thanked her for taking the clothes off the line or warming his chair for him! There was simply no justice in the world for ordinary dogs, only Labradors.

Seeing how sad Holly looked, Mac had a change of heart. "Okay," he said, "I'll take you for a walk, but I'm still mad at you."

Chapter 2

Holly Goes Wild!

Mac's anger began to disappear as he walked onto the street with Holly. He felt calmer with every step.

Up ahead, Mr. Jones, the bank manager, was coming out of the bank. His dog, Curly, trotted proudly beside him. Unfortunately, Curly was a Labrador. And Holly disliked any Labrador.

Holly went wild. She barked and snapped at the Labrador's heels before crouching down and making scary growling noises.

Suddenly Holly launched herself at Curly
like a canine cannonball. Curly jumped
into Mr. Jones's arms. He toppled over and
fell backward, with his dog on top of him.

Mac grabbed Holly and held her back.

"Is this your dog?" boomed Mr. Jones, his voice dripping with rage.

Mac hesitated for a moment before saying, "I'm afraid so . . . sorry."

The banker struggled to his feet. "Well, you should keep her off the streets. She's a danger to society."

"No, she isn't," Mac protested. "She just doesn't like Labradors."

But Mr. Jones wouldn't listen. "And furthermore," he continued, "you can forget about that bank loan you applied for. If you can't be trusted with a dog, you can't be trusted with the bank's money. Good-bye!"

Mr. Jones and his dog strode away.

Mac slumped against the wall. "That's not fair."

When Holly put up her paw to shake hands, he pushed her away.

"This is your fault. If you hadn't picked on the banker's dog, I would have gotten that loan. If I had any sense, I'd take you back to the dog pound."

Chapter 3

The Chase

Holly was just an ordinary dog. She couldn't understand what Mac was saying, but she had heard the words "dog pound" before. That's where Mac had found her when she was a puppy. Dog pounds scared her. She stared into Mac's eyes and saw only anger.

So Holly ran . . . and ran . . .

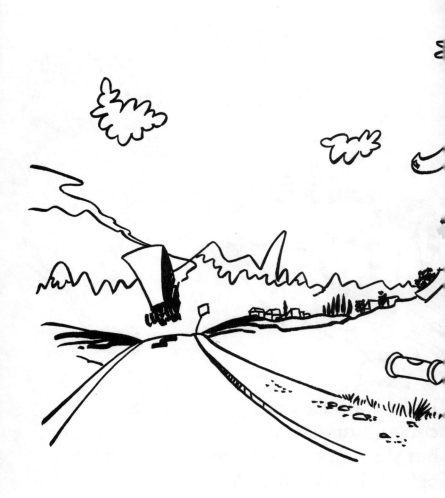

She was streaking down the street when she
went whack! — straight into a mail carrier.

It was an accident, but unfortunately, it was the mail carrier's first day on the job. She thought Mac was attacking her. She scrambled up a tree.

Letters fluttered through the air as Holly took off again.

All Holly wanted to do was to get home and stay out of trouble.

But as she rounded a corner, she saw
another Labrador out for a stroll.

Mac had threatened to trade her in for a Labrador. It was her run-in with the bank manager's Labrador, Curly, that had made Mac so mad at her. Holly closed her eyes, opened her mouth, and charged at the Labrador.

The Labrador moved aside at the last second and Holly plowed into a man delivering eggs.

Suddenly there were scrambled eggs everywhere!

Now the Labrador dared her to charge again. Holly torpedoed ahead, but the other dog again dodged out of the way.

Holly missed the Labrador, but accidentally
crashed into a ladder that a little boy was
climbing.

As the boy was about to fall into the wet cement, Sergeant Sam Costello turned the corner, made a frantic dive, and caught him just in time.

The sergeant grabbed two passing police officers. "Let's get that dog!" he shouted.

By this time, Mac had forgiven Holly and was running through the streets calling her name.

Holly was still chasing the Labrador. And Mac, the police, the mail carrier, the little boy's parents, and the egg man were all chasing Holly.

On and on the chase went. Holly ran as fast as she could, but she couldn't get near the other dog. The Labrador was a genius at twisting and turning, and an expert at making an ordinary dog look silly.

While trying to catch the Labrador, Holly splashed through wet cement,

upset a fruit stand,

knocked over a man on stilts,

scared a man on the sidewalk playing music
so much that he almost swallowed his flute,

sent a group of boys running in ten
different directions, and . . .

completely demolished the Unbreakable
Homes Company's build-it-yourself home
display.

This exhausting chase and demolition derby was at last starting to tire the amazing Labrador. It was also wearing down Mac, the police, the mail carrier, the little boy's parents, and the egg man.

Chapter 4

You're Under Arrest!

But Holly, as plucky as the pluckiest of dogs, was still raring to go.

When she saw the Labrador leaning against the side of a building to catch her breath, Holly made a desperate lunge.

The Labrador ducked and Holly flew past
her and—Oh, no!—sent a nun flying!
Holly landed in the nun's lap.

Dazed and winded, Holly clambered to her feet. She was about to resume the chase when Sergeant Costello grabbed her collar. "You're under arrest!" he exclaimed.

The other officers, the little boy's parents, the mail carrier, and the egg man were all huffing and puffing and fussing over the nun.

"Whoever owns this dog is in serious trouble!" Sergeant Costello bellowed.

Then Mac, barely able to walk, hobbled up. "Her name's Holly, and she's mine. I'll pay for all the damages somehow — just don't hurt her."

Holly made a little whimpering sound and Mac gave her a hug.

"That dog chased me up a tree!" shouted the mail carrier.

"It tipped over the ladder my little boy was on!" yelled the boy's father.

"I lost dozens of eggs because of that mutt," growled the egg man.

By now, Mr. Jones, the banker, was on the scene. "No one's safe with that dog around," he said. "It should be locked up in the pound!"

Mac drew Holly close. "You'll have to lock me up first. This dog is my only friend."

"Then you'll have to get another friend," Sergeant Costello declared.

The police were about to lead Mac and Holly away when a group of people cautiously sneaked out of a nearby building and onto the street.

"That's her!" shouted a young woman. "She's not a nun!"

"Quick! Grab her! She just robbed our bank!" screamed a bank teller.

"She's not a nun!" cried an old lady.

The fake nun jumped to her feet and
started running. But the police tackled her.
As they wrestled her to the ground, bundles
of money flew into the air.

"It's a man! It's Daring Dudley Lurksmith!" Sergeant Costello grinned.

"He always uses disguises for robberies," said a police officer. "Last week he pretended to be an astronaut, and the week before that he wore a clown suit. Today he pretends to be a nun!"

"Too bad!" growled Dudley Lurksmith. "Disguising myself as a nun could have been a profitable habit."

They were about to take Daring Dud to jail when Sergeant Costello looked across at the Labrador that Holly had been chasing. It was too tired to move after all that running.

The sergeant grinned again. "This is our lucky day! It's Lefty, Daring Dud's crooked canine accomplice. Take that dog away, too!"

"We've been looking for Lefty and Dud for ages," Sergeant Costello explained. "While Dud robbed the banks, Lefty acted as watchdog and barked if the police came around."

The sergeant patted Holly's head. "This is a pretty smart dog. It must have known that the Labrador was a crook."

Even Mr. Jones had to agree. After all, it was *his* bank that Daring Dud had tried to rob.

"Well done," he told Holly. Then he turned to Mac. "I've changed my mind about that loan. Come and see me tomorrow."

"What about all the damage the dog caused?" asked the egg man.

"The damage can be paid for out of the reward money," said Mr. Jones.

"You mean I get a reward?" Mac spluttered.

"Of course you do," said the banker. "You've saved us a fortune."

"Your dog is a hero," declared Sergeant Costello. "If I have my way, Holly will receive a medal!"

Later, as Holly and Mac walked home, Mac said, "I wasn't *really* going to trade you in for a Labrador. And I will never put you in a dog pound. I promise!"

Holly stopped walking and put up her paw to shake hands. This time Mac didn't push her away.

About the Author

Bill Condon
Bill Condon decided to write *Holly & Mac* because he knows a lot about dogs. In fact, as a child, his favorite foods were dog biscuits and old bones. He had to give them up when he found himself barking at cats and chasing them.

Bill spends his days fetching the paper and chasing a ball. He has also had about forty children's books published.

About the Illustrator

Gus Gordon
Gus Gordon is a freelance cartoonist and illustrator based in Sydney, Australia. He draws for a variety of magazines, teaches cartooning, and serves on the Australian Black and White Cartoonists Club committee.

As a young man, Gus worked on cattle stations around Australia. He attended Agricultural College for a while — where he found himself continuously drawing "silly" pictures. So, he left to become a cartoonist.

Gus loves illustrating children's books. He also enjoys surfing, rugby, and listening to weird music.